A Christmas Panorama

THE FRIENDLY BEASTS
&
A PARTRIDGE IN A PEAR TREE

Illuminated by VIRGINIA PARSONS with calligraphy by Sheila Waters

DOUBLEDAY & COMPANY INC. GARDEN CITY NEW YORK

PRINTED IN HOLLAND 1966

ISBN: 0-385-11453-2 TRADE
0-385-11454-0 PREBOUND
PRINTED IN THE UNITED STATES OF AMERICA

THE FRIENDLY BEASTS

JESUS our brother kind and good.

Was humbly born in a stable rude.

And the friendly beasts around Him stood
Jesus our brother, kind and good.

'I'said the donkey, shaggy and brown.
'I carried His mother up hill and down,

"I carried her safely to Bethlehem town;
I," said the donkey, shaggy and brown.

'I' said the cow, all white and red,
    'I gave Him my manger for His bed.

'I gave Him my hay to pillow His head;
I,' said the cow, all white and red.

'I' said the sheep, with the curly horn,
  'I gave Him my wool for His blanket warm;

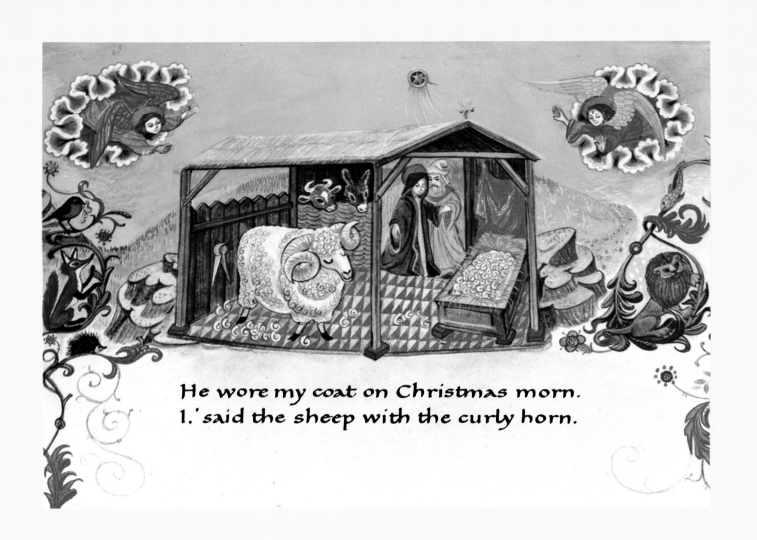

He wore my coat on Christmas morn.
'1,' said the sheep with the curly horn.

'I'said the dove, from the rafters high,
'Cooed Him to sleep, my mate and I,

We cooed Him to sleep, my mate and I;
I, said the dove, from the rafters high.

'I' said the dog, with the dark brown eyes,
   'I kept watch under darkening skies,
    Watched over Him until morning's rise,
    I,' said the dog, with the dark brown eyes.

And every beast, by some good spell,
In the stable dark, was glad to tell,

Of the gift he gave Emmanuel,

The gift he gave Emmanuel.

A PARTRIDGE IN A PEARTREE

On the First day of Christmas
My true love sent to me

A Partridge in a Pear Tree

On the Second day of Christmas
My true love sent to me

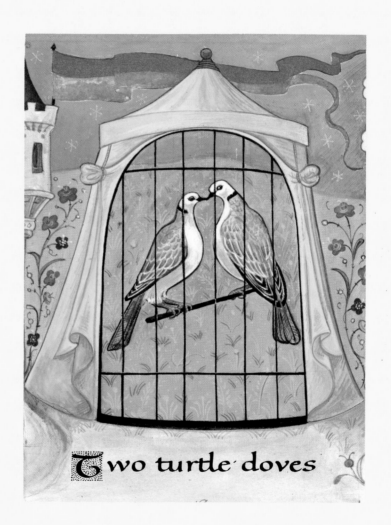

wo turtle doves

and a partridge in a pear tree.

On the Third day of Christmas
My true love sent to me

hree French hens

two turtle doves
and a partridge in a pear tree.

On the Fourth day of Christmas
My true love sent to me

Four colly birds

four colly birds,
three french hens,
two turtle doves,

and a partridge
in a pear tree:

On the Sixth day of Christmas

My true love sent to me

Six geese a-laying

five gold rings,

two turtle doves,

four colly birds,

and a partridge

three french hens,

in a pear tree!

On the Seventh day of Christmas
My true love sent to me

Seven swans a-swimming

six geese a-laying,
five gold rings,
four colly birds,
three french hens,

two turtle doves,
and a partridge
in a pear tree.

On the Eighth day of Christmas
My true love sent to me

Eight maids a-milking

seven swans a-swimming,

six geese a-laying,

five gold rings,

four colly birds,

three french hens,

two turtle doves,

and a partridge

in a pear tree.

On the Ninth day of Christmas

My true love sent to me

Nine ladies dancing

eight maids a-milking,
seven swans a-swimming,
six geese a-laying,
five gold rings,
four colly birds,

three french hens
two turtle doves,
and a partridge
in a pear tree.

On the Tenth day of Christmas
My true love sent to me

Ten lords a-leaping

nine ladies dancing,
eight maids a-milking,
seven swans a-swimming,
six geese a-laying,
five gold rings,

four colly birds,
three french hens,
two turtle doves,
and a partridge
in a pear tree.

On the Eleventh day of Christmas
My true love sent to me

Eleven pipers piping

ten lords a-leaping,
nine ladies dancing,
eight maids a-milking,
seven swans a-swimming,
six geese a-laying,

five gold rings,
four colly birds,
three french hens,
two turtle doves,
and a partridge in
a pear tree.

On the Twelfth day of Christmas
My true love sent to me

welve drummers drumming

Eleven pipers piping
Ten lords a-leaping
Nine ladies dancing
Eight maids a-milking
Seven swans a-swimming
Six geese a-laying

Five gold rings
Four colly birds
Three french hens
Two turtle doves
And a partridge
in a pear tree